FOUR-THREE-TWO-ONE...

tic Four

FOUR-THREE-TWO-ONE...

Writer:
Paul Tobin
Artists:
Vicenc Villagrasa, Pere Perez & Denis Medri
Colors: **Sotocolor's Andrew Dalhouse**
Letterer: **Blambot's Nate Piekos**
Cover Artists: **Clayton Henry & Guru eFX; David Williams & Guillem Mari; Jon Buran & Chris Sotomayor; and Roger Cruz & Chris Sotomayor**
Consulting Editor: **Ralph Macchio**
Editor: **Nate Cosby**

Collection Editor: **Jennifer Grünwald**
Editorial Assistant: **Alex Starbuck**
Assistant Editors: **Cory Levine & John Denning**
Editor, Special Projects: **Mark D. Beazley**
Senior Editor, Special Projects: **Jeff Youngquist**
Senior Vice President of Sales: **David Gabriel**

Editor in Chief: **Joe Quesada**
Publisher: **Dan Buckley**
Executive Producer: **Alan Fine**

#45
·2008·

Who would'da ever thought a fight against the Frightful Four would go so danged well?

Yes...even with Doctor Doom leading them, their defeat took mere moments.

Revenge! I'll have my revenge!!
I didn't even get a chance to flame on.

Ack, ack, ACK!!
And it's all thanks to our new team leader--

MORDECAI MIDAS,
the richest, swellest, **dreamiest** guy on Earth!

Yes. Midas leads the **Fantastic Five** like a **dream!**

Everything's been **dreamy** since **he** joined the **FF!**

And what a **dreamboat** he is!

BRIIING BRIIING

Mordecai?

IF YOU CAN'T JOIN THEM-- BUY THEM!

PAUL TOBIN - WRITER VICENC VILLAGRASA - ARTIST
SOTOCOLOR'S A. DALHOUSE - COLORIST
BLAMBOT'S NATE PIEKOS - LETTERER
HENRY & GURU - COVER ANTHONY DIAL - PRODUCTION
RALPH MACCHIO - CONSULTING NATHAN COSBY - EDITOR
JOE QUESADA - EDITOR IN CHIEF DAN BUCKLEY - PUBLISHER

BRIIING
Mordecai!
BRIIING
Midas!
C'mon, c'mon! What does it take--
--to wake you up?
Huh?! What is--? Snort Snuffle
Oh. I see.
Were you having the dream again?
Yes. The dream. Always the dream! I simply must join the Fantastic Four!
And it's time to make my dream a reality.
Why is this so important to you?

Publicity, of course.
We business magnates have endured horrid public relations of late, and joining the world's most popular family would do wonders for my image.
And I would naturally take on the role of financial advisor to the Fantastic Five.
Meaning I could patent, and reap rewards from, all the technology that Richards is currently simply...uggh...giving to humanity.
So, how do you plan to join them?
A cash offer should certainly suffice.
They don't seem like the type you can buy.
Ahh, Madame Masque, there are NO types that cannot be bought.
"But if that unthinkable scenario should actually occur, then I would see to it that I saved them from some nefarious villain.
"Once they saw how truly heroic I am, they would beg me to join!"
And if no villains show up at a timely moment?
Hah! With you on my pay there is no fear of that!

MANHATTAN.
ONE WEEK LATER.
Quoth the raven, try my store!
RED RAVEN
What are you looking for, Sue?

try my store!
RAVEN
Any works by **outsider** artists. Bizarre folk art. Weird paintings. That sort of thing.

I like to find out about the artist. Do **research** on their **lives,** try to discover who they were.
I'm slowly convincing Reed to fund an **art museum.**

How about you, Millie? Looking for anything in particular?
Vintage clothes. **Especially** anything from the **1920s,** or the **1960s.**

Sometimes I find a **real** treasure.
Once I found a dress actually **worn** by **Twiggy** during the photo shoot for--

Susan Storm! What a coincidence!
Umm, yeah.
Isn't that Mordecai Midas?
≈Sigh≈ Yes. He's been pestering us of late. Wants to join our team.
Join the team? Of course! I can do much to further the cause!
For instance, I saw you two pretty ladies looking over this establishment's merchandise.
So I bought the whole store for you! It's yours, Susan!
Ms. Storm, please. And why would we want the whole store?
Yeah...we were just looking.
But, it's yours, now!
Don't you understand? All YOURS!

Quoth the raven, try my store!
RED RAVEN
This jewelry? YOURS! These dresses? All YOURS!
Uh-huh.
Why didn't you just go with shiny trinkets and moving objects?
But, don't you, I mean-- hmmm.
CLIK
KRISH
Oh no! It's Madame Masque! A super-villain!
ZEEEEEEEENN
Madame Masque? What are you doing--here?
Yeah! What's up with attacking an antique store?
I--umm...I heard there's--an--ancient Pre-Columbian Roman Emperor tiara here!
One that could give me--extra arms.
Extra arms?

Oh, never mind my reasons!
Stay back, Millie! She's dangerous!
Dangerous is right!
Too dangerous even for you, Susan!
I'll take charge of--
Ch-Chump
KRASH!
Eff!
Look out!
THOOMP
Should've kept your eyes on me, Madame Masque!

Me too! Millie the Model isn't the kind of girl who just stands around looking pretty!
Oh... wait.
Look out! She's getting away!
Huh? I am?
Oh, yes! Right!
Another day, Susan Storm! Farewell!
Well, that was kind of strange. I've always heard that Madame Masque is efficient and deadly, but she mostly seemed... confused.
Perhaps she didn't expect me, and it frightened her.
Yeah... maybe.
RAVEN
Antiqu
Oh well, I'll be in touch.
With an offer to join the team?
Hardly. To bill you for all the broken pottery. It is my shop now.

ONE DAY LATER.
And so I obtained this rare sports car as a gift for you.
Wow! Thanks!
So I was thinking--
Hmm-hmm! Check out those girls! I kind of like the cosplay look!
You enjoy fashion? I know a fashion distributor that--
Say, I didn't know the Gears were playing tonight. Maybe I should go?
THE GEARS
I could easily obtai backstage--
Apartment House of the Undead: Part Two?! It's already out?!
Awesome!!
Will you pay attention?!
Apartment Ho the Undead: Pa

A DAY LATER...
I suppose this machinery you've had delivered could be somewhat useful, perhaps as raw materials for my experiments.
Raw materials?
But these devices are the leading edge of current technology!
Are they?
Hmmm. They seem primitive.
Besides, even if it were true, what would be the point?
The point would be that you wouldn't have to waste your time making things.
You'd already have things! Powerful things!
But it's not that I want to have highly advanced items of technology. I want to make them.
I'm researching because I love research, not because I want power. Do you understand?
No?

A DAY LATER...
UFFF!
Kid! You okay?!
Just got the wind knocked out of me!
Ben! Look out for the--
FBANG
Dreadnoughts? Is that what you were going to say?
Too late, pretty boy! My dreadnoughts cannot be stopped!

This isn't looking good, Ben.
Awww, I seen worse. They're just robots.
We'll find a way. It's what we do. Because we're the--

FANTASTIC FIVE!
The what?
Midas, again?
Oh no! It's the Mighty Midas!

The Mighty Midas? Who calls him that?
Villains everywhere, that's who! They know that--
OOF!

THUNK

He's knocked out!
Protect him!
And save me that sandwich! Smashing a robot horde always makes me hungry!

Uhhh--
Oh no! Before he saved that child by taking the laser blast that knocked him unconscious, Midas heroically sprayed my dreadnoughts with Dissolvo-X!
Laser blast? Child? Dissolvo-X?

Yes! Dissolvo-X, the one thing that could...eat up their... circuitry, maybe, to, umm--
--to cause a short that would turn my own robots against me! Curse you, Midas! You win!

That was a weird fight. How's Midas?
I think he's coming around. Maybe I should wave an ice cream cone beneath his nose or something--
Uhhn--

Did I, uhh, save you? Did we win?
You tripped and fell.
No seismic readings on that yet, but I'm guessing they felt it in Iowa.

Yes. Of course. Make fun of me. Fine. I'm used to it.
You can't know what it's like to be ridiculed just because you're huge and misshapen.
Maybe he can't, but I can.
Sorry, that Johnny's such a--
Handsome guy? That's true. So you guys can stay here. Clean up. Have yourselves a sulk-party.
But I've got a date.

Is he always a jerk?
Naww. Sometimes he's worse.
Well, I, sir, need something to eat. Come now, I'm buying.
That's for me!
MONDAY.
These are great seats!
Enjoy them! And the food's complimentary.
TUESDAY.
Hah! This is fun! Ain't never had a chance to do this before!
Most boats don't have enough pull to let a guy like me water-ski!
I know how you feel!
You know, Mighty Midas, it might be that you do.

VEDNESDAY.
You see, r all my great alth, for all that e attained in the iness world, I'm ill judged almost entirely by my appearance.
I hear that.
THURSDAY.
It's a stigma. People expect me to be a monster, just because I look like one.
Right! Same here. And now... it's clobberin'-- dang it!
FRIDAY.
You know... perhaps it's too late for me. Maybe I am a monster. But, you, Ben. Maybe my billions could help.
Maybe my scientists could find a cure for your condition. Would you like that?
Maybe. Yeah... maybe.
But I have to tell ya, Midas, all s is interesting, but ue ain't never going to let you join the Fantastic Four.
Not unless something really dramatic happens.
What will be, will be. It's not really important to me.
Is he falling for it?
I believe so. Time for the next stage of our plans.

SATURDAY.
There are...a...lot of...them!
Hold on, Susie! I'm coming!
What now, Thing Fight me, and m dreadnoughts destroy you!
Fight them, and I will have the honor of your annihilation!
Don't give yerself any medals just yet...cuz, sister, ol' Benjy's still swinging!
Fire's not working!
Don't go any hotter! There are too many nearby buildings!
AAARGH!
For now, maybe! But we're wearing you down! You know it! I know it!
This is the end of the Fantastic Four! There is no one who can save you!

No one? We'll see about that!
No! It's Midas!
Have a taste of this neutronic-ray! Developed by my very own scientists!
No! You've disrupting their circuitry! Just when victory was in my grasp!
With Midas here, I'm lucky to escape!

Except, you're not escaping.
What? Nets?!
Sue's plan is working. Perfectly.
What's going on?
Did you think we were idiots? Hello? World's best brain, right here!

World's best leader, right here.
World's most cheese-covered pretzel, right here.

Ben, these past few days? Were you just--?
Playing you? Yeah.
Madame Masque escaped after the first two fights. We needed to draw her out one more time.
No. There was more. More than just a trap for Madame Masque.
I can judge a man, sir, and some of the things I was saying--

Look, your plan to join us was ridiculous anyway, because the bottom line is that the Fantastic Four is a family.
Yeah...FF stands for Fantastic Four, but it could stand for Family, First.
Or Freaky Friday, I guess.

Have fun in prison!
Sue, you took an awful chance, drawing Madame Masque out like this.
Those dreadnoughts had a big helping of nasty coming to 'em.

Had to do it, though.
Why's that? We coulda found Madame Masque some other way.
True, but you so enjoy destroying robots. I couldn't take that away from you.

Haw, thanks Sue. Sometimes I--
Mommy, lookie! Why's that man so weird? Is it acne? Is it monster acne, Mommy?

I'm soooo sorry.
Awww, don't worry 'bout it. Just kids.

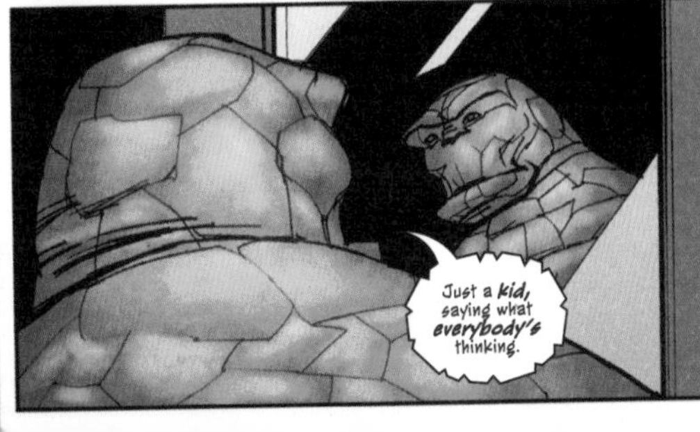
Just a kid, saying what everybody's thinking.

KRRSH
Ben!
Ben, you can't just--
Back off, sis.
Johnny, I--
Shut up. Listen.
No matter what you do, some people will judge you by your looks. Just keep it in mind that it's better to be thought of as a monster, than to actually be one, like Midas.
I know, Johnny. It's just... sometimes--
Awww, nuts. I better go inside and pay for this window.
Wait, Ben.
This one's on the family.
THE END.

#46

NEW YORK CITY.
I can't believe it! A 1949 Mercury Monterey!
Wonder who owns it? Wonder if they'd like to--

Ugghh!

WHABAM
Oofff!
It's the YEAST that I can do!

Flame on, sucker! Nobody gets the drop on Johnny Storm and gets away with--
RRRRRRR
What the--? What are you?

Whoa!
Too late to dodge the car! But I can't melt it! It's too cool!
Get down!

Wha--? Sue? Where did you come from?!
Never mind that! Pay attention to the fight, little brother!
A TIMELY FAMILY APPEARANCE
PAUL TOBIN-WRITER PERE PEREZ-ARTIST
SOTOCOLOR'S DALHOUSE-COLORIST
BLAMBOT'S NATE PIEKOS-LETTERER
WILLIAMS & MARI-COVER JOE SABINO-PRODUCTION
RALPH MACCHIO-CONSULTING NATHAN COSBY-EDITOR
JOE QUESADA-EDITOR IN CHIEF DAN BUCKLEY-PUBLISHER
ALAN FINE-EXECUTIVE PRODUCER
During an experimental rocket mission, four crew members were bombarded with cosmic rays, granting them weird and amazing abilities. They are explorers, adventurers, imaginauts. They are the FANTASTIC FOUR.

Little brother? Where did that come from?
From the bottom of my heart!

I watched this thing leap out at you, but you were paying so much attention to a car that you were oblivious!
URRR?
Wait...you were watching me? For how long?

Ummm...well... just an hour or so.
What?! Are you kidding?!
Hey! You get into so much trouble, sometimes it just pays to keep tabs on you!
URRK!

I can't believe this!
And I can't believe you're letting that thing get away!

Dang! That thing is fast!
Well, if you would have kept your mind on--

Shut up.
What?
You know what? I've had it.
Lately you've been on my case about everything. And now I find out you're spying on me? It's too much!
Johnny, I--
I need my space!
I'm moving out of the Baxter Building!
Johnny?

LATER.
Johnny... you sure you're wanting to do this?
I think it's time, Ben.

Maybe. But we're kinda family, you know?
How could I not know? Lately, Sue has been all about "little brother" this and "little brother" that.

We've had some tough scrapes in the past few months. Makes some people think. Take stock of the people you love.
Sue's just worried abo you.

I hear that. In fact, I hear that all the time.
Well, a man's gotta do what a man's gotta do, even if he is a flamin' hothead idiot that's doing the wrong gol-danged thing.

Say... whose place is this, anyway?
Don't exactly look like no hotel.

It's Jane Hastings's apartment. A friend of mine.
She's off on a tour of Africa. Asked me to watch her place for a couple weeks.

Good enough.
Take care, Johnny. Don't be a stranger.

Cuz you're like my little brother, too.

MONDAY.

TUESDAY.
PERFECT STORM

WEDNESDAY.

THURSDAY.
--odd results on the tests from the hairs Sue gathered from that creature the two of you fought.
Dude...I do not like it when you say things are odd.
KITTY

Not only did the creature have a totally unique structu
I'm frankly not sur if it was organic.
MISHINA
Come again?

It seems to have been made out of, well, to put it simply--colored ink.
Weird. Keep me updated. Sue still doesn't know where I'm at, right?
No. Ben and I won't tell her. But --
Gotta go. Thanks, Reed.

FRIDAY.
--and then I threw all the pasta in his face.
Totally deserved it. Wish I could have been there.
Me too, squirt. I mean... Johnny.

SATURDAY.
Yo! Johnny Storm, here.
WE KNOW WHO YOU ARE, JOHNNY STORM.
Huh? Wow. Your voice is squeaky. Who is this?
THIS IS SOMEONE WHO OWES YOU A VERY SINCERE APOLOGY FOR TOUGHY TOMCAT.

For what? Did you just say Toughy Tomcat?

WE DID. TOUGHY TOMCAT IS THE CREATURE THAT ATTACKED YOU LAST WEEK, AND I'M AFRAID HE DID SO BECAUSE OF...US.
WOULD YOU LIKE TO MEET, AND TALK ABOUT THAT?
You're dang right I would! This Toughy Tomcat thing almost took my head off!
THEN IT'S SETTLED. COME TO THE MCGRAW-HILL BUILDING AT 330 WEST 42nd STREET, PENTHOUSE SUITE, IN ONE HOUR.
AND PLEASE BRING THE REST OF THE FANTASTIC FOUR.
Toughy Tomcat, huh? And what was up with that guy's squeaky voice?
Well, I suppose I should call Ben and Reed. And Sue.
Naw...I can handle this alone.

SOON.
Dude... why doesn't anyone put addresses on the tops of buildings?

Then I'd never have to land.
Lots of buildings have heliports. Why don't they have a landing area for--
Whoa!!

Huh?

You again!

RRRRRRR
So, Toughy Tomcat's your name, huh?
Well, try this on for size, and if you don't like it, that's just tough, cat!

Hah! That put a little damper on your plans, didn't it?

POP
What the--?!

Yikes!

SHWOOSH

Okay, maybe this time you'll!--

POP
What? Hey! No grabbing!

It's a
Look at that thing!
What is it?

Unnghh!

Running off again? Why?
It wasn't anything I did. Unless it got tired of beating me up.

You okay, Johnny?
Huh?
Oh...great. Now you're keeping tabs on me?

I thought you guys were going to respect my privacy.
Yeah, well, when I hear a police report of some flaming guy fighting a werewolf, I can't just change the channel and listen ta Mozart.

For what it's worth, I coulda been here quicker, but I gave you some space.
Thanks for that, I suppose. Still...my private life--
Stop.
Huh?

I said stop. If this is going to turn into some whine-fest, I'm the wrong guy.
If you want to get your own apartment and eat pizza alone, that's your business. But if you want to fight weird menaces in freakin' downtown New York, well, then it becomes my business. Got that?
Ben, I--

And as far as privacy, when you want to be alone, you can just flame off and disappear into a crowd.
I ain't exactly got that option, do I?

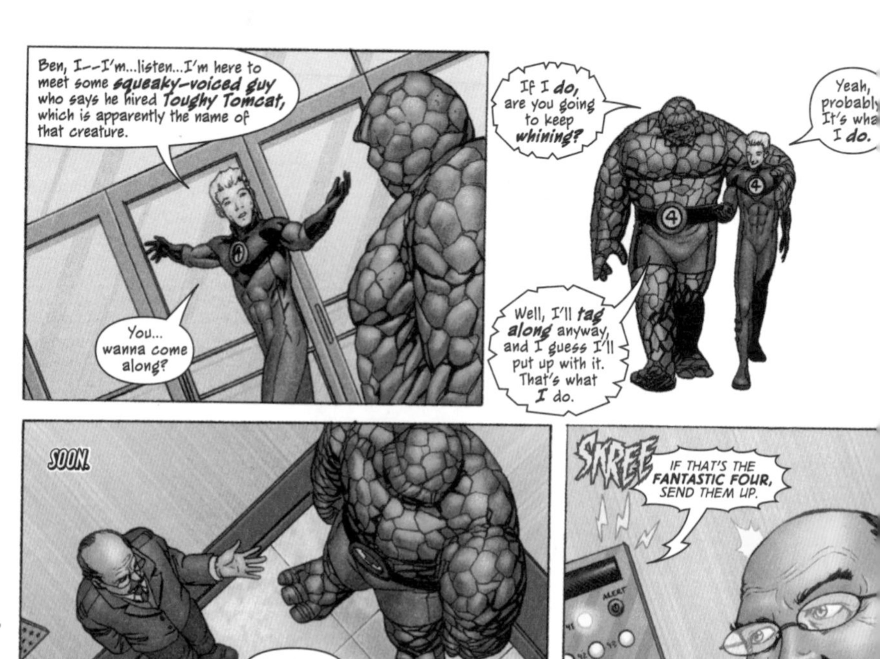
Ben, I--I'm...listen...I'm here to meet some squeaky-voiced guy who says he hired Toughy Tomcat, which is apparently the name of that creature.
You... wanna come along?
If I do, are you going to keep whining?
Yeah, probabl It's wha I do.
Well, I'll tag along anyway, and I guess I'll put up with it. That's what I do.

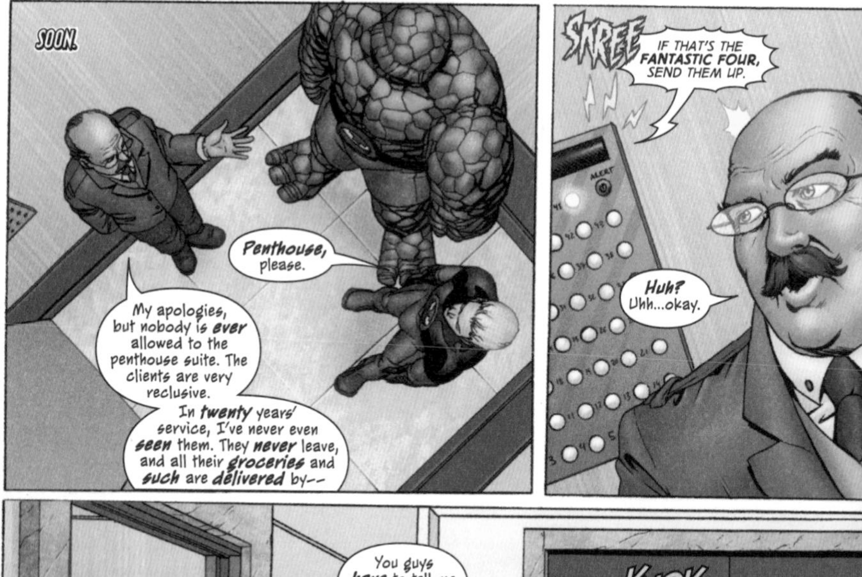
SOON.
Penthouse, please.
My apologies, but nobody is ever allowed to the penthouse suite. The clients are very reclusive.
In twenty years' service, I've never even seen them. They never leave, and all their groceries and such are delivered by--
SKREE
IF THAT'S THE FANTASTIC FOUR, SEND THEM UP.
Huh? Uhh...okay.

You guys have to tell me what these guys look like!
I've wanted to know for years!
KNOK KNOCK

Be ready for anything.
I am. If these guys actually did hire that werewolf cat-creature, no telling what other strangeness--

HELLO, HELLO, HELLO!
SUPER RABBIT
--could be around.
WELCOME, WELCOME, WELCOME!

I'M ZIGGY PIG. THIS IS SILLY SEAL. AND YES, WE'RE CARTOON CHARACTERS.
COME IN. SIT DOWN. WE'LL TELL YOU OUR STORY.
"IT BEGAN IN THE 1940'S. WE WERE PRETTY POPULAR IN THOSE DAYS.
1

"BUT THE FAME DIDN'T LAST, AND SOON WE WERE LIVING OFF DWINDLING CARTOON ROYALTIES.
"THERE DIDN'T SEEM TO BE ANY PLACE FOR US IN THE MODERN WORLD.
"TOUGHY TOMCAT WANTED TO PROVIDE FOR US. PROTECT US.
"HE STARTED TAKING BOUNTY HUNTER JOBS, FEELING THAT HIS FELINE SIDE WOULD HELP HIM TRACK DOWN HIS PREY.
"HE GOT REALLY GOOD AT IT. AND HE CHANGED.
"MAYBE HE WAS JUST CHANGING WITH THE TIMES.
"THE MONEY WAS GOOD, BUT TOUGHY BECAME TOO PROTECTIVE. WE HAVEN'T LEFT THESE APARTMENTS FOR DECADES.
"TOUGHY SAYS THE MODERN WORLD IS TOO DANGEROUS.

"BUT **WE** WERE GROWING UP TOO. NO LONGER SATISFIED WITH OUR WAY OF LIFE.
"WE WANT OUR FREEDOM. WE **NEED** IT."

TOUGHY WON'T **LISTEN** TO US, THOUGH. IF WE LEAVE THE APARTMENTS, HE **TRACKS** US DOWN, **CATCHES** US, BRINGS US HOME.
HOME? IT'S MORE LIKE A **CAGE!!**

SUPER RABBIT
S
AND TOUGHY'S **JOBS,** I'M NOT SURE THEY'RE ALL...**LEGAL** ANYMORE.
I FEEL LIKE **WE** HAVE TO **SAVE HIM!**

SO WE CAME UP WITH A PLAN. A **DUMB** ONE.
YEAH...WE **SECRETLY** HIRED TOUGHY TO **TAKE DOWN,** ummm...THE FANTASTIC FOUR.
Z
You what??!

WE DIDN'T THINK THERE WAS **ANY WAY** HE COULD **DO IT!**
WE THOUGHT HE'D LOSE **BAD,** AND THEN MAYBE **LEARN** THAT DOING **EVERYTHING** YOURSELF, SHOULDERING **EVERYONE'S** RESPONSIBILITIES, **DOESN'T WORK!**
THEN HE'D START TO INCLUDE **US** IN THE CARTOON **DECISION-MAKING.**

Okay then... you guys screwed up, but we can fix this.
We gotta find this Toughy Tomcat character, make him listen to reason.

When we find him, let me do the talking.
I said we gotta make him listen to reason, not get super-model dating tips or--

Yikes!!
BLAM

RRRRR
The epic search comes to an end.
Yeah... I guess it makes sense he'd be around here, keeping an eye on the pig and the seal.
I can't believe I just said that.

Now, let me handle this. Gotta make him listen to reason.

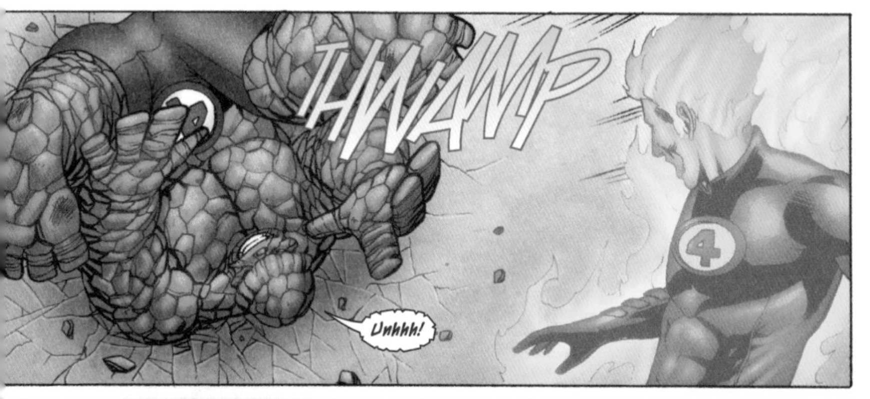
THWAMP
Unhhh!

That's IT!
You just gave me a reason to whap yer skull around!

You better hope you got nine lives, Toughy, cuz I'm about to smack eight of 'em into orbit!

Ben! I don't think this is going to work!

Seems to have worked just fine. Let's get him upright and we'll--
RRRRRRRR
POP
Dang!
He's doing it again!
PIANO PATROL! MOVING, TUNING, RESTORATION
I'm gonna just keep hammering at him! He has to have his limits!
Maybe. But I'm not even sure we should be fighting him!
Listen, Toughy! I know how you feel! But I know how Ziggy and Silly feel too! You have to let them have their own lives!
Okay... this time yer gonna stay down!
Your friends have to live for themselves! Are you listening?
POP
Wha--? Again?
If you don't let them take some chances, fight a few of their own battles, they'll never learn!

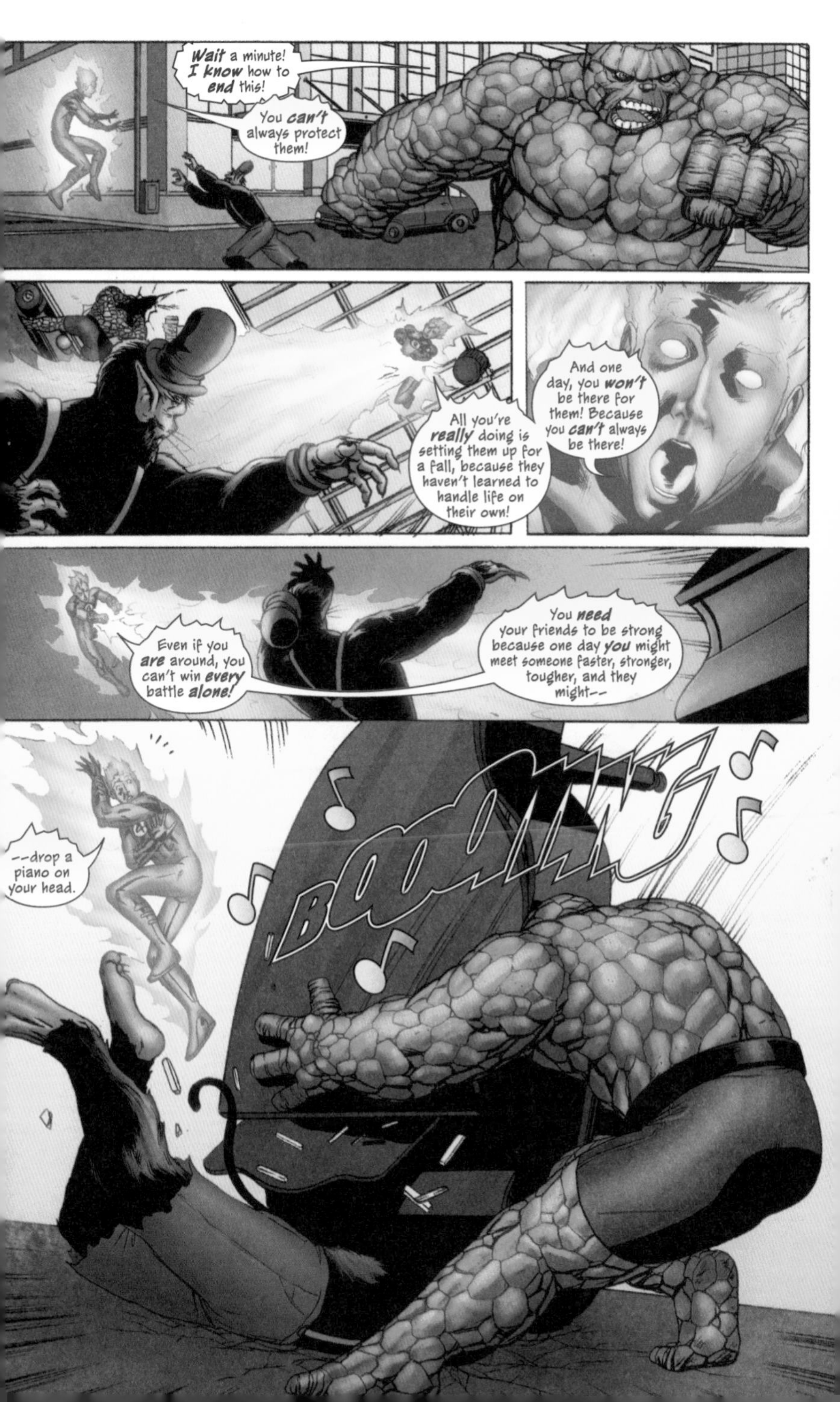
Wait a minute! I know how to end this!
You can't always protect them!
All you're really doing is setting them up for a fall, because they haven't learned to handle life on their own!
And one day, you won't be there for them! Because you can't always be there!
Even if you are around, you can't win every battle alone!
You need your friends to be strong because one day you might meet someone faster, stronger, tougher, and they might--
--drop a piano on your head.
BOOIIING

There. That always stops 'em in the cartoons.
Ya got that right.

Huh. Look.
He's changing.

YOU'RE BACK!
HI'YA, BUD!
GOSH! I'M SORRY, GUYS!
THAT MATCHSTICK GUY MADE SENSE. I WUZ BEING A JERK.

Aww, IT'S OKAY.
WE KNOWS YA WUZ ONLY DOING IT CAUSE YOU LOVED US.
I guess now I know a little more about how Sue feels.

And I guess I know a little more about how you feel.
YIII!

Reed! Sue! You were-- listening?
Yes. For several minutes now.
We heard about the battle, and we came as fast as we could because--
--uh, not that we didn't think you could handle it, but--

It's okay, sis. I love you too.
Huh?

Thanks, Johnny. You ever going to move back to the Baxter Building? I miss you.
I suppose I miss you too. Soon as my friend Janet comes back from Africa, I'll be coming back home.

SUNDAY
CRADDLE OF CHIPS
COOKIES ALOT!
BACON BITS
Hmmm.

Not those. They're really bad for you!
Yiiiii!
CHEESE REX
CHEESE SNACKS

Sue!
Sorry!
Sorry!
Sorry!
Sorry!
CLAK
CLAK
CLIK
CLAK
CLIK
CLIK
THE END.

#47

ANHATTAN.
Just...stay... calm.
S.W.A.T.
NYPD
POLICE
We can't risk a Hulk incident, here. Lot of people could get hurt.
I understand. We'll do what we can.
Why does everybody always tell me to stay calm?!
Can't you understand how angry that makes me?
S.W.A.T.
Can you guys handle this if he goes green on us?
Heck, yeah!
Maybe.
Maybe not.
Just... want...to be left... alone!
No! It's too late! I'm...urrrr... changing!

Ben! Just keep cool!

Ben? There is no Ben Grimm!! Not anymore!

Now there is only...the INCREDIBLE HULK!

Usually the Fantastic Four are a family that was bombarded with cosmic rays and given weird and amazing abilities. But...no one seems to be themselves right now...

THE TERRIFIC TRIO IN...

GRIMM SMASH!

PAUL TOBIN -- WRITER VICENC VILLAGRASA -- ARTIST SOTOCOLOR'S A .DALHOUSE -- COLORIST BLAMBOT'S NATE PIEKOS -- LETTERER
BURAN & SOTOMAYOR -- COVER REV. PAUL ACERIOS -- PRODUCTION RALPH MACCHIO -- CONSULTING NATHAN COSBY -- EDITOR
JOE QUESADA -- EDITOR IN CHIEF DAN BUCKLEY -- PUBLISHER ALAN FINE -- EXECUTIVE PRODUCTER

Leave me alone! Arghh!
That's it! Let's put him down! Flame on!
Careful, Susan!
Oh yeah! Time for the Hulk to feel the heat!
Hah! Going for a little carnage, were you?
Get it? Car-nage? It's 'cause you're throwing a car!
Less of the jokes, Susan. We've got a job here, and every second we let this continue is another opportunity for tragedy to strike!
When I see Ben like this, I can't help but think it already has.
"I can remember how it all started, years ago.

"The three of us going into space aboard the experimental rocket.
"Ben was scheduled to be our pilot, but was called away at the last moment to be an observer for an important army experiment...the gamma bomb.
"And while our shielding was failing, accidentally bathing us in cosmic rays--
"--Ben had problems of his own, saving young Jean Summers from the gamma bomb explosion."
"Ben was a hero, but it cost him dearly. He became the creature known as the Incredible Hulk!
I can't control him anymore! The Hulk has gone berserk!

"While we ourselves became the Terrific Trio!"
I can't help but think what would have happened if Ben had come with us!
This monster would have never been born!
There will always be a Hulk! Always!
Susan! Get some firebolts in the Hulk's face!
They don't hurt him!
That's not their purpose! We just need him momentarily blinded!

FWOOSH
ARGH!
This will give me a chance to get in close enough!
And now I can cut off his air supply! Render him unconscious!
AGHH!
Hulk hate stupid stretchy man!
John! Get away from him! He's too powerful!
I always-- UNNHH-- underestimate his strength! It's incalculable!
Get out of there, John! Oh dude...this is bad!
Hulk!
Huh? Hulk hear stupid voice?

Calm yourself, my friend. There is **no need** for **violence.** No need to be **angry.**
Hulk not... angry?

What's happening?
Look! It's the **X-Men!**

I believe **Professor Doom** is using his mental powers to calm **Ben.**
Whatever.
All **I** care about is meeting **Marvel Girl** and the **Phoenix!**
Looks like **somebody else** needs to be **calmed down.**
HAA HA HA HA!

Thanks for your help, Professor Doom.
Always a pleasure to use my powers for the greater good.

We can take over from here.
Thanks, Mike.
You know his name?

Of course. We X-Men work closely with the military and the New York police.
It's the least we can do, since the government has been so generous in their support of mutants.

Victor!
Victor Von Doom!
Over here!
Over here!

CLIK
FLASH!

LATER...
«Terrific Trio and X-Men join forces to halt the Hulk.»
So, Susan... the military has your friend Ben under sedation now?

Yes. Unfortunately, the military is the only organization with the facilities to contain him. I only hope we can visit him.
I'll contact General Peter Parker for you. He's an old friend.
You have friends in the U.S. army, Natasha?

Of course. I mean, sure, in my Black Widow days I was a Russian spy...but that doesn't matter much.
All the world's agents get to know each other. It's like athletes in sports...someone who plays for the Red Sox can still be friends with a Yankee.

That's blasphemy, Natasha.
Ha ha! Okay, maybe that's a bad example.
But anyway, I haven't worked for the Russians since I was bitten by that radioactive spider, and started my new life as the Black Spider.

Where's Reed, by the way?
He and John went shopping for clothes. Why...are you interested?
What can I say? I like 'em a little goofy.

Would it bother you if I asked him out?
Of course not. He's just a friend.
And I couldn't possibly be interested in a man right now. My experiments take up too much of my time.
Really? What are you working on these days?
A string harmonizer.
Huh? Sounds like a musical instrument. I thought you only worked on the big brainy stuff.

This is for the strings that comprise all universal dense matter.
Oh. So, not a guitar, huh?
There's been something wrong with the universe lately. A background hum.

Somebody blew out the speakers?
No. I mean there are discordant notes, completely out of sync with the way things should be. Something's wrong.

You'll figure it out and fix it, Sue. You always do.
This one's complicated. I might need to call in a magician.
Let me know how it all works out. Meanwhile, since you don't mind, Reed Richards and I will be hitting the clubs.

LATER THAT NIGHT, AT THE BAXTER BUILDING.
Thank you for helping.
I could do no less, Susan. Not when the Terrific Trio requests the aid of Norrin Radd--
--the Sorcerer Supreme!
Thank you, Norrin. Now then... my string harmonizer is--
It sounds like a musical instrument.
I already did that joke. Go on, Susan.
Right. Utilizing a neutrino paradigm constant as a guide and gauging an odd displacement of their proper oscillation between muon, electron and tau status--
Whoa! Whoa! English, please.
Susan, you are hurting our brains.
Here... I made a funky television.
Wow...this will revolutionize, umm, ugly appliances. Now if we just had repulsive refrigerators and hideous washing machines the world would be--
It's receiving displaced signals.
This thing gets bad reception.
The signals are displaced from reality. Out of sync.
Coming from another continuum?
No, it's definitely from ours. But...not quite.

And why am I here?
To use your strange powers to boost the signal.
Dr. Norrin Radd. Sorcerer Supreme and television repairman. Get your toolbox, doc.

Hmm... I'll see what I can do.

ZZZZZZRRZZZZZZRRRZZZZZ

--rrrrllo? Hello? Yes! We're getting through!
Hi from the Fantastic Four!

It's...us. The Terrific Trio. Except, who's that with us?
Huh? Me? I'm the Thing. Ben Grimm. At yer service.

Ben Grimm? The Thing? Ben Grimm is the Hulk.
It's as I feared.
What do you mean?

Someone or some thing is playing with reality. Should I fail to resolve this in time, all reality might be rewritten.
How odd.
Reed sounds... smart.
That is kinda strange.

So what can we do from our side?
I'm sending out these messages as a fail-safe. It's possible that I won't be able to fully resolve this attack on reality before I myself am... restructured.
But, you can follow on with the task, using my research in order to get this mission accomplished.
Should we trust him?
I think so. Yes. My own research has been leading to these same conjectures.
Plus, Reed's even more attractive when he's smart.

Hey!
It's just that I feel... something... that...
What? I thought you didn't like him anyway.

Rrrgh! Send me that research material.
Absolutely. Using a cosmic positioning system, I've discovered an anomaly focal point at coordinate 66-890-432-9-4398--

--674-2202-097. According to that...umm, weirdly intelligent Reed, this is where the problem is coming from.
Not sensing evilness.

Now let's just see what we're looking at.
What's that thing?
Right now I'm using it as a reality emission detector. It should enable us to see objects and space as they were before reality began its odd fluctuations.

Hmm. There's a door.
A door?
Yes. And... oh my.

What?
It's us. We're all changed in some way.

We'd better get through this door and see what's really going on.

Where are we?
Huh?

And who's that?
Down, Reed.
But his question was one I think we all share. Who are you?
I'm the Keeper.
THWIP
Well, you could keep me if--urrk!

Here...you dropped some of your puzzle pieces.
Should I just--? Hey, wait.

Susan, look at these.

You're doing all this, aren't you?
Umm, all what?
Playing with reality. Changing things around.

These puzzle pieces. Is this... reality?
Stop playing around! The Celestials sent you to stop me, didn't they?
Ummm... yes. Yes. They did!
So anyway, you might as well admit it!
What are you talking about? We aren't-- Urkk!
THWIP
Fine. Whatever. I got bored, okay?
Who wouldn't get bored?
"I've been doing this for like, nine billion years!
"Endlessly keeping watch on reality. Making sure that such and such piece is in just its proper place, that everything connects seamlessly, and that all the pictures match."
But it's booooring!

So I was playing around a little. Changing a piece here and there. Putting them into different alignments.
What's it really matter?
It matters because you're playing with our lives.
Your lives? But nothing I've done should have...
Wait a second.

You're not from the Celestials at all, are you?
Grab her!

I got her! I'll try to hold her, but she's incredibly--

Hmm. I can hold her, easy. She's not powerful at all.
Well why should I be? I mean, I'm basically just a normal girl.

Nice. Everything went easy for once.
Keep her still, and we'll try to get these pieces figured out. Just make sure the Keeper doesn't try any--

THWAMM
--tricks.
The pieces just got all mixed up!
Whoa.

HA HA HAAAA!
I'm multi-armed, and dangerous!
SMAK
Unff!
What? Where'd they come from?!

unnnnh. I'm...okay.
Dude! This reeks!
SRRP
SRRP
SRRP

FLAME ON!!!
Look out, Susan!

Thanks, John!

We need to get on the offense!

BOONK
No! We'll take care of the offense! You guys can just take a chair!
It's no good! We're off balance! They're hitting us too hard!
It's too bad...urg...we don't have a great big strong Thing, like that Fantastic Four team we were talking with!
WHISH
WHISH
HA HA HA! These will put you underground!

THOOM
Uhhnn! Too strong!
Suzie!
Dudes, can we talk about this?
This is bad.
John! Where are you?

Me? Oh, I'm just putting a puzzle together.
Just about finished, actually.
click
We're back!
Oh dang it!

The villains just disappeared! You did it!
Yeah. I figured the real problem wasn't the bad guys, or the Keeper, it was that puzzle.
And I'm good at games.
In fact, if you're free some night, I've got some puzzles, board games, video games, or--
Or nothing. I lose. You win. Go away.
SNAP

Wow. We're suddenly home in the Baxter Building.
That was one major league cold shoulder that Keeper girl tossed your way, Johnny.
No big deal. Win some, lose some.

And as far as saving reality, like the pretty lady said, we win this one.
Do we? I wonder...who keeps the Keeper? Who's to say she doesn't just do this all over again?

No problem. I... umm...borrowed a couple of the pieces.
Well done, Matchstick. Well done.
THE END.

#48

NYC.
JohnnyOnFire Having some chow at that taco stand @SisterSue told me about. What are you guys doing?
Agent M TACOS
OrangeRock Just got through fighting Man Mountain Marko. Wasn't exactly a fight, though. And he wasn't exactly a mountain.
IQ313 Fight's over? So then it's...Man Molehill Marked Off?
Thank you for making it to the opera, Reed. Even if you did have to project your hologram.
Sorry. I can't really interrupt my experiment right now, but I didn't want you to get lonely.

THE END OF TIME.
During an experimental rocket mission, four crew members were bombarded with cosmic rays, granting them weird and amazing abilities. They are explorers, adventurers, imaginauts. They are the FANTASTIC FOUR.
MOVING DAY
PAUL TOBIN – WRITER DENIS MEDRI – ARTIST SOTOCOLOR – COLORIST
BLAMBOT'S NATE PIEKOS –LETTERER CRUZ & SOTOMAYOR –COVER PAUL ACERIOS – PRODUCTION
RALPH MACCHIO – CONSULTING NATHAN COSBY – EDITOR JOE QUESADA – EDITOR IN CHIEF
DAN BUCKLEY – PUBLISHER ALAN FINE – EXECUTIVE PRODUCER

THE PRESENT.
JohnnyOnFire Sorry everyone! Have to go fight some BDR. (JohnnyOnFire has signed out)
Metallo has come to your puny planet! This world is now mine!!
Reed, do you think we could go on vacation soon?
If you like. My current experiments are portable.
What are they?
Nano-aircraft.
Yeah. That sounds portable.
Would you like to go to the coast? The mountains?
Anywhere is fine. It's just always nice when we can spend some time together.
Johnny, are you blogging on a social network during battle?
Well...yeah. I have to stay in touch with my fans.
JohnnyOnFire Note to @IwouldmarryJohnny and @FlamedOn...a "BDR" is a Big Dumb Robot.

THE NEXT FEW DAYS...
Hey, Sue... I'm at the grocery store.
Didn't you say you needed some yogurt or something?
Johnny. I was thinking about the Gears concert tonight.
You wanna call whichever girl you're seeing lately? Make it a double date?
Thanks for coming shopping with us, Ben.
We girls are too dainty to carry everything we buy.
I think the Hulk is too dainty to carry everything you ladies buy.
He's cute when he pretends to be grouchy.
I find myself jealous of your team, Susan. It's like a family.
I'm not pretending!
Oh, we are a family. I honestly don't ever have to feel alone.
Susan, can I buy the complete Basil Rathbone Sherlock Holmes DVD set?
DVDen

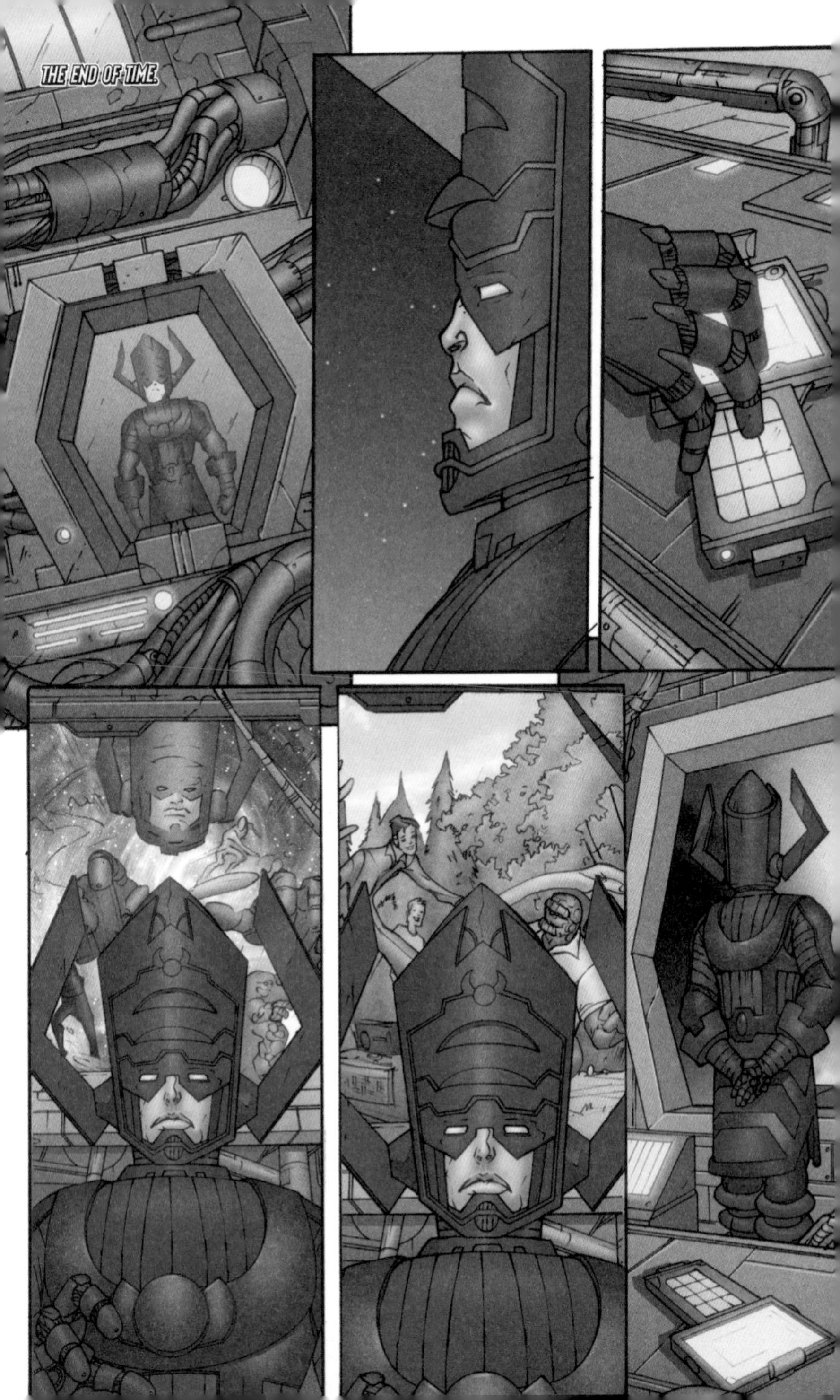
THE END OF TIME.

THE PRESENT DAY.
Reed Richards, did you call just to talk to me?
THE END OF TIME.
THE PRESENT DAY.
I picked up enough football tickets for all of us.
Yes! I love soccer!
Wait, is this soccer football, or football football?
Date tonight, Johnny?
Naww. I thought I'd just stay in. Hang with you guys.
THE END OF TIME.

THE PRESENT.
So should we order out for pasta? My stomach demands some of the fettuccine that we--
Just a moment.
BEEP BEEP BEEP
Hello? Richards. This is...
...GALACTUS.
Shorter than I remember.
He must be adjusting the hologram to meet us face-to-face.
Strange. That's kind of... not arrogant.
Though it pains one such as myself to ask for aid, I find myself in dire need of your assistance.
Will you lend me your powers?
For what purpose?
I am... moving.
You need help packing? Need somebody with a truck?
I don't get it.

I vote we **help.**
Why? This guy **EATS planets.**
We can't judge a being like Galactus, and--
And you ain't the type'a guy who says **"no"** when somebody needs help. Okay, let's put on our **tin stars** and **white hats** and help out the Big G.
Okay. We'll **help** you, but if what you're **doing** is--
--wrong?
Now where are we?
You stand at the **End of Time.** I have transported you **billions** of years into the **future.**
Dang! And **you're** the guy what needs help **moving?**
Out there, the universe is **collapsing.** Soon, all will be **gone.**
I cannot stay.

"As you know, I am a being of the universe which predates your own.
"Then too, I witnessed the end of all time.
"But through science beyond even your quite estimable minds, I was able to escape oblivion. To survive.
"I am the last vestige of the universe before this one, and I shall survive yet again.
"Though universes may die, Galactus will live on."
Why do you need our help? You've done this once; surely you can duplicate the process?
I can, but there are those who would stop me, and my preparations are exacting. I can have no distractions.
Sounds to me like you're asking us to fight your battles for you.
Precisely.

A cult known as the Black End has dedicated themselves to preventing me from moving on to the next universe.
They believe that as the universe falls, then too should all things.
My belief is that it is not philosophy which drives the Black End, but spite.
They are bitter that they have no means to continue on, while I myself shall maintain my existence.
These Black End chumps, anybody we know?
"Possibly. I believe you are acquainted with Annihilus, though perhaps not his current state.
"And while you know the Silver Surfer, you know not of the being who stole his powers.
"The much-diminished Kree Supreme Intelligence is a member of the Black End cult.
"As is the Air-Walker, an automaton of my own sad making.
"The leader of the Black End is Kratos, a child of Thanos, who himself fell to the forces of the Shi'ar in the Final Skrull War.

Sounds like you're expecting us to step up to the plate against the League of All Stars.
Should you agree to this, I would lend you a great deal of my power. It would, I expect, be sufficient.
I need your promise that in the next universe you will restrict your diet to uninhabited worlds.
Agreed.
Well?
Okay. Let's do this.

I am sending you to one of the last remaining planets in the universe.
There, the Black End are preparing an assault that would doom me to perish along with this universe.
And what's this funky hunk o' metal?
Its name is Zero. It functions as a power conduit, from myself to you four.
When it is near, your own powers will be immensely heightened.
Does it have a stereo?
Good question. Nothing like a little mariachi music when going into battle at the end of the universe.
No. My apologies. There is no music.
We wuz only kidding, high hat. See ya' in a bit.
FZZZTTT
What is this madness?
Company's here! Who's for a game of cards?

Ahhh. I understand. This must be some desperate ploy from Galactus.
Indeed. And a pitiful one at that.
Ahhh, my foes of old, come here to vanish with the rest of us. With all of us.
So, nobody wants to play cards? Texas hold 'em? Five card stud? Go fish?
Johnny... hush.
We do come from Galactus.
He wishes no war between you.
He wishes to leave us behind to our doom!
We will not allow him to continue!
Not when our demise is certain!
Seems like an ego thing to me.
Not now, Ben.
Hey, it's the end of the universe. This might be my last chance to mouth off.
This doesn't have to end with a fight.
Perhaps not, but it does have to end, and we might as well end with a bang.
Bang.

SHRAAK
Hmmpfff. Impressive.
Sue?
That wasn't even difficult. It must be Galactus's added powers.
Really? Wonder what I can do?
FLAME ON!
I feel kinda... big.
Big?

Yeah. Big.
A fire attack? Hah! My defenses will--
FWOOSHH
KRAGGK!
Now I see what you're talking 'bout, Johnny.
Yeah. Big. Scratch one robot.
So let's see what I can do with this power boost.
Cretin. I am of the stars.
A thousand of you could not move me so much as an inch.
An inch, huh? How's about a few yards, Chuckles?!
WATHOOM
Ugghhh! That's impossible!!
What is this?!
The machine! They're drawing power from the machine! Destroy it!

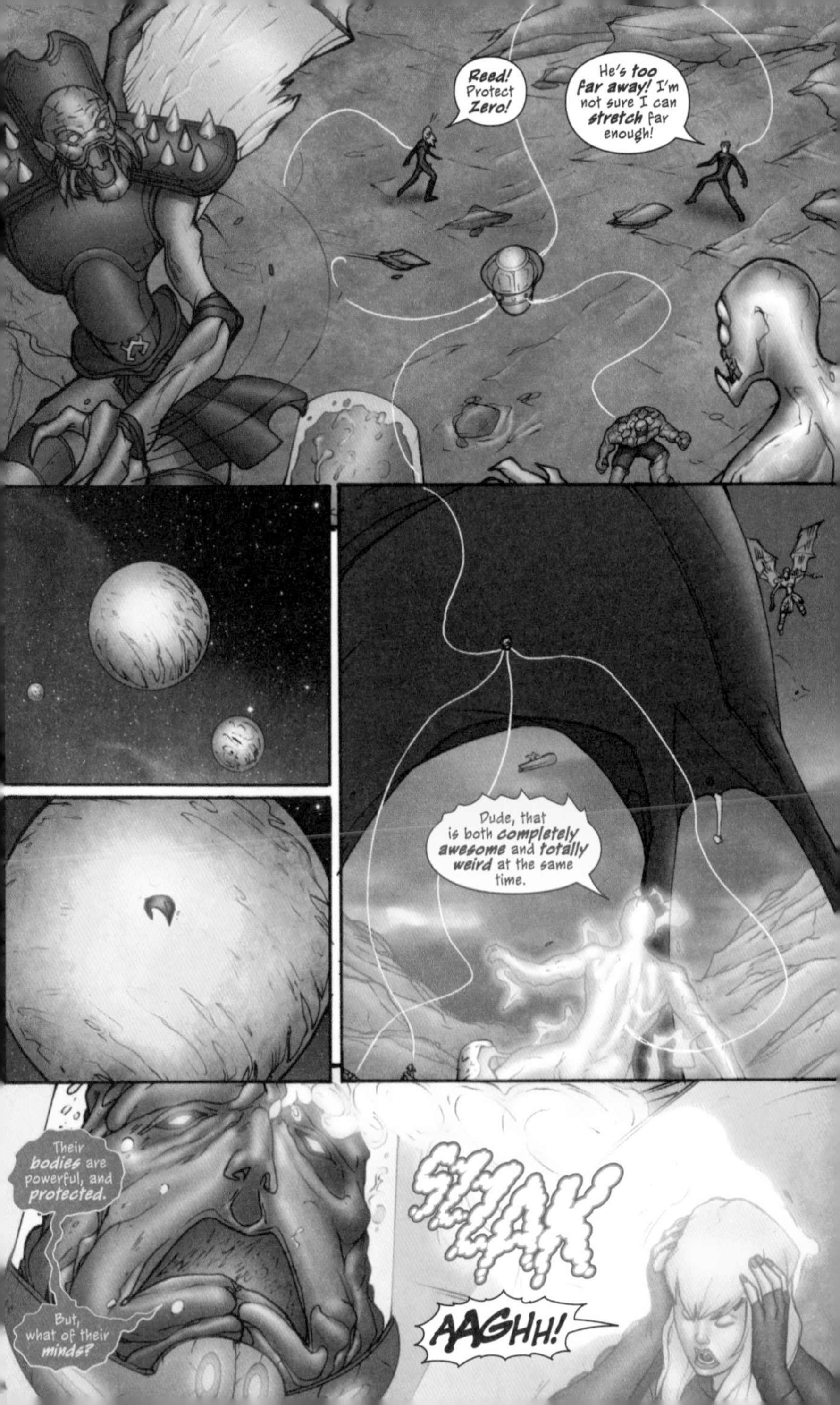
Reed! Protect Zero!
He's too far away! I'm not sure I can stretch far enough!
Dude, that is both completely awesome and totally weird at the same time.
Their bodies are powerful, and protected.
But, what of their minds?
SKZAK
AAGHH!

Unnnff!!
Sue!
That blow should have been sufficient. No human could have possibly--
KRUNCH
What?
Looks like you idiots will keep underestimating us humans all the way up to the end of time!
Works for me! I like being the underdog!
Oopsie. I broke your toy.
I've got you, sis! I'll protect you!

Stay back, unless you want a taste of flame!
I wield the Power Cosmic, fool!
Let's play chicken!
Sweet. I'm wielding the power Galactus!
There.
I... warned... you...
...that--
Unggh.
Johnny?

Ben! This isn't going well!
Sue and Johnny are down and I'm having difficultly controlling my added powers!
Retreat is a viable option.
Huh? You talk?
Get us out of here!
ZVIIIP
They're fleeing!
Back to Galactus, most likely. We must follow!
The End of Time is now our time.
VOOPP
Galactus!
Hmmm?
They were too powerful! We had no choice but to retreat!
And lead them to me, no doubt.

Yes!! Prepare for--
No doubt, indeed.
FWUMPH
Astonishing. You simply--
I did nothing but return them to their lands.
This failing universe will have them soon enough.

And now my final preparations are complete and I must--
Explain why you needed us at all? Yeah...that'd be nice!
Those Black End knuckleheads weren't even bumps in your road!
Johnny. Ben. Be quiet. Galactus has his own reasons.
Huh?
But we--
Reed's right.
But we should be going back to our own time, now.
Granted.

Yes. I'll miss you, too.

THE PRESENT.
WIB
And I still don't know why the Big G came running to us, I mean--
Johnny... clue in.
Huh?
Wait a minute. I think I got it.
Galactus didn't need us to fight his battles.
He was just... lonely.
You've got to be kidding!
"Kidding? Not at all.
"He's been an outcast for several billion years. And for him, it's about to get even worse.
"He's traveling to the birth of a brand new universe. Can you imagine the huge weight of being the only creature in all creation?
"It would be an unbearable burden to be so completely, and entirely...
"...alone."
THE END.